First published in this edition 1976
Published by William Collins Sons and Company Limited, Glasgow and London
© 1974 Centro Internazionale del Libro S.p.A., Florence
© 1976 English language text, William Collins Sons and Company Limited
Printed in Great Britain
ISBN 0 00 138137 7

LEONARDO DA VINCI'S
FANTASTIC ANIMALS

Interpreted and
transcribed by
Bruno Nardini

English language
text by
David Grant

Illustrated by
Adriana Saviozzi Mazza

Introduction by
Isabel Quigly

Collins
Glasgow and London

Contents

INTRODUCTION

The Notebooks of Leonardo da Vinci make wonderful reading, whether you dip into them for immediate excitement or pore carefully over one of their sections. What they contain has been called "the records of the mightiest machine perhaps that has ever been a human brain." Leonardo wrote down much of what he observed, thought and imagined, and he illustrated his ideas and observations with detailed sketches.

He wrote about nature in all its forms—in the working of the human body, in animals, in plants and in the earth. Everything that lived and grew or had lived and grown in the past excited him : the movement of birds or water or wind, the anatomy of the brain, the behaviour of the weather, flight, weight, geology, geography, botany, astronomy. He wrote about

Left: the da Vinci castle, with its bell tower, and turret, known as the "quarter-deck", in a rare etching by Telemaco Signorini.

Right: a costume designed by Leonardo, which shows the influence on him of the Italian painter and sculptor, Andrea del Verrocchio.

man-made things as well: architecture, canals, warfare, the techniques of painting. And, more extraordinarily perhaps, he wrote about what might happen in the future.

Leonardo was able to imagine, in a remarkably detailed way, all kinds of inventions that only appeared hundreds of years after his death—machines that would bring both progress and destruction, like the aeroplane and the tank. He foresaw what would happen not just in the case of mechanical inventions but in all sorts of fields of knowledge, in physics and optics, for instance, and he understood far better than anyone else in his day or for a long time after it, things which only much later became clear to scientists, things like the circulation of the blood.

Left: it is traditionally believed that the adolescent Leonardo was the model for Verrocchio's famous *David*.

Right: a depiction of Florence towards the end of the 15th century.

But although he was such a careful investigator, and so passionately interested in the minutest detail of things in nature, he was an artist as well, which means he interpreted that world and did not just record what he saw there. His imagination was able to create not just an exact and likely future, but worlds of fantasy in which strange creatures lived and fabulous things happened.

These worlds were never separate from the world he actually observed and touched. Leonardo believed in the unity of all things. His scientific investigations were touched with fantasy, his most fantastic stories are filled with a sense of the truth of the imagination.

One of the most remarkable drawings in the Notebooks is a "study for a monster." It is of a

Left : Leonardo's fantastic imagination found full expression in his depiction of strange animals.

Right : nature was, for Leonardo, the "school of truth".

human foot showing every vein and muscle with perfect exactness, but with bear's claws in place of toes. This shows the method he used in telling many of his stories. The creatures he describes may be mythical beasts like the phoenix, which is burnt to death yet always rises from the ashes, or the basilisk, which kills whatever looks at it or comes near it. They are products of his search for truth in every form, including poetic forms in which parables and fables tell us hidden truths. And even his most fantastic creatures are wonderfully vivid and easy to imagine.

Most of the stories are not about monsters and legends, though, but about everyday animals that can teach lessons of patience and faithfulness and love, sometimes of cunning and cruelty : owl, hawk and

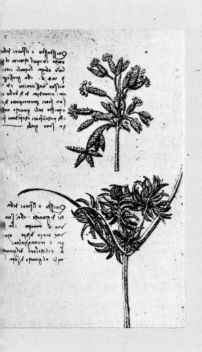

Two different views of the human face: the ugly exterior seen from the side, as in the caricatures on the left; and the inner truth, shown in the gentle face of this young girl on the right.

turtle-dove, pigeon, falcon and goldfinch, cocks and hens, bats, bees, spiders, snakes like the asp and the viper, impressive beasts like the lion and the panther, homely ones like the mouse, the duck and the donkey. All of them and their brief stories, which Leonardo took mostly from ancient sources, tell us something of the workings of nature.

Some of them are funny, some sad, some realistic and some fabulous. These divisions do not matter. All are minutely observed by an artist and thinker who saw all aspects of life as one, who longed to unite the worlds of fact and fantasy, of the mind and the imagination, the man-made and the natural.

Even Leonardo's own gifts overlapped. Although known chiefly as a painter and sculptor, he believed

13

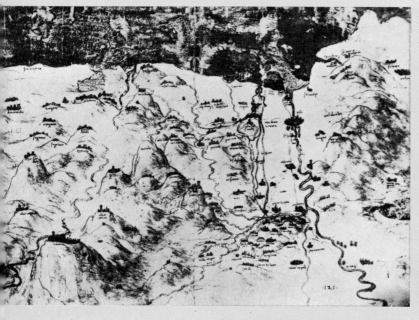

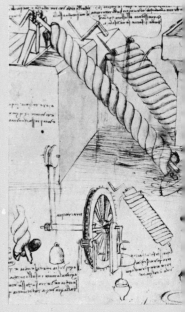

Left: a relief map of the Arno valley between Arezzo and Florence.

Right: the "hydraulic engineer" is an appropriate title for Leonardo, who anticipated the technical advances of our own age.

strongly in the power of the written word and spent much of his life writing down his ideas. In his day, pens were made out of quills—the feathers of birds with one end sharpened into a nib. "Feathers shall raise men as they do birds, towards heaven," he wrote, "that is, by letters written with their quills."

Isabel Quigly

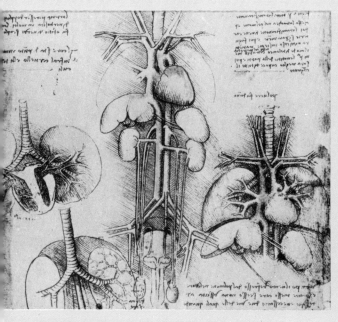

Left: anticipating the work of the Belgian anatomist, Andreas Vesalius, Leonardo dissected and described the human body in a splendid series of anatomical drawings.

Right: a view of the Mugello valley from above Scarperia.

FOREWORD

In Leonardo da Vinci's writings, information about the man himself is rare. We have to look for his soul and his art at the point where, we might say, fantasy and scientific observation merge.

Leonardo was the poet of daily life who clothed everyday things in fantasy and beauty. He was the observer of nature who knew the hidden virtues of plants and the secret habits of animals; and he was also the storyteller with his legends about nature.

There is nothing new in portraying animals which think, speak and act like humans. The telling of fables, using this form, has always had a place of honour in European literature.

Here we come to the delicate issue of Leonardo's sources. In 1883, the scholar Jean Paul Richter collected and published in London the literary works of Leonardo. These served as the basis of all research. In Italy, however, it was declared scandalous, and it was said that Leonardo had merely copied medieval writers. It is known that his library contained more than one hundred volumes, including Aesop's Fables. He intended to compile a great compendium of books examining, among other things, ancient wisdom as revealed in fables.

The pages of this book contain the essence of popular wisdom from the provinces of Valdarno and Mugello, gathered and put onto paper by Leonardo da Vinci.

Bruno Nardini

FANTASTIC ANIMALS

The phoenix

While the phoenix was flying between the desert and the sea, she saw a camp fire in the distance. She knew that the time of her great trial had come. Now was the time to have faith. She must calmly accept her fate.

For a time, she hovered solemnly on motionless, outstretched wings. Then slowly she began her circling descent.

The phoenix was bigger than any eagle. And she was more beautiful too, with her vivid plumage.

As she neared the ground, she could feel the hot air from the fire fan her feathers. Without a moment's hesitation, she flew straight into the heart of the flames.

Later, as the fire died down, a small blue flame flickered among the embers. It grew brighter and bigger, and rose into the air spreading out as if it had wings. This was the phoenix being reborn from her own ashes to live in the sky for another five hundred years.

The owls and the hare

Two owls, perched in a tree, were watching a hare run about a field.

"Poor creature," said one of the owls. "She doesn't even have the courage to return to her form."

"Why not?" asked the other owl.

"Because she is afraid . . ."

"Afraid of going into her own home?"

"That's how it is with the hare," replied the owl who had spoken first. "She lives out her whole life in fear. Now that summer is past, and the leaves are falling, she dares not even look at the trees. She rushes backwards and forwards, terrified by this golden rain falling all around her."

"How cowardly she must be!"

"Yes. And running about like that she will certainly end up in some trap, or be shot by hunters."

The chameleon
and the hawks

When the hawks flew out of the clouds into clear blue air, they saw a small creature high above them. Naturally their pride was wounded, and they set off in pursuit. But soon they were out of breath and had to fly back down to a lower level where the air was not so thin. They stretched their wings and rested.

The strange creature they had seen was blue as the sky. It seemed to be studded with jewels when the sun splashed it with golden rays.

As the hawks circled among the clouds, they saw their quarry again. But it was not blue now. This time it was a mixture of white and grey, just like the clouds.

It flew around them and they called, "Who are you?"

"I am the chameleon," came the reply.

"And where do you come from?" asked the hawks.

"From everywhere," replied the chameleon. "I live in the air, in the sky. To find peace, I fly high above the clouds where the air is so thin that no bird can follow me."

As it spoke, the chameleon flew out of the clouds. At once, it shone again brilliant blue and gold.

The hawks were worn out trying to keep up with this mysterious, constantly changing creature. Finally they gave up the chase and spread their wings like surrendering soldiers.

"You cannot fly at this height," called back the chameleon, "if you were not born up here."

As suddenly as it had appeared, it was gone.

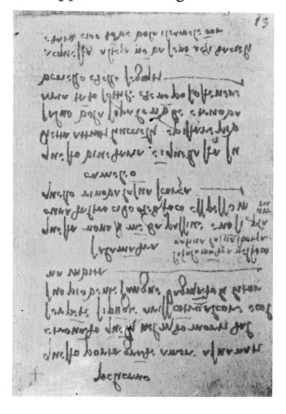

The turtle doves

A male turtle dove and a female turtle dove lived together for many years in a little wooden dovecote which the farmer had built for them. They were never apart, whether flying, eating or sleeping, and were a truly devoted couple.

In the spring, many a male dove tried to win the beautiful female by challenging her mate. But she remained faithful, even when he was defeated in the struggle for her.

One day, the female saw that something was wrong with her mate. His feathers were ruffled, and he could not hold himself upright.

"You must be sick," said the female to the male. And she flew off into the wood to look for medicinal herbs.

When she returned, the dovecote was empty. The male was dead, and the farmer had already buried him.

The female wept for a long time. Then she made a vow. She would remain chaste for the rest of her life, faithful to the memory of her dead mate. Never again would she come to rest on a green branch or drink clean water.

Ingratitude

"How devoted those pigeons are," said the farmer's dog one day, as he looked up at the dovecote.

"They are always together, kissing and murmuring to one another—not like down here in the henhouse, where there is nothing but fights and quarrels."

"What a fool you are," said the cockerel, who was perched on a cart. "You don't understand pigeons at all, do you? When they are very young, they show the greatest tenderness and respect towards their parents. But when they grow up and can fend for themselves, do you know what they do then? I'll tell you. They turn on their father and fight with him, until finally they drive him away from the nest.

"And worse than that, they steal his wife from him, forgetting that she is their mother. So you see, pigeons are really the most ungrateful of birds."

26

The cow and the snake

One day, a huge boa constrictor slid into a field where a cow was grazing. He slithered through the grass towards her, and slowly wound his coils round her legs. Then he squeezed so hard that the cow was quite unable to move.

Then the reptile slid his head under the cow's belly and began to suck her milk.

When he had drunk his fill, the snake loosened his grip and slipped away. The poor cow was very weak and fell to the ground.

Snakes love milk. They can smell it from a long way off and will travel great distances to find it.

The falcon and the goldfinches

When the falcon returned from hunting, he found to his astonishment that two goldfinches had settled in his nest beside his young.

He was in a very bad mood. Hunting had not gone well that day. He had only found carrion, and falcons would rather starve than eat rotting meat.

He flew into a rage when he saw the goldfinches in his nest. He just managed to stop himself seizing hold of them. He could not kill them; they were far too small.

The goldfinches were terrified. They huddled together trembling and hardly even daring to breathe.

"What are you doing up here?" the falcon demanded indignantly.

"We are lost," cheeped one of the goldfinches in a tiny frightened voice.

The great bird of prey looked at the intruders with fierce eyes. Although he and his babies were hungry, he could not bring himself to eat the goldfinches.

So he shouted, "Get out! Go home!"

As the little birds flew off as fast as they could, the falcon said to his young, "The falcon only eats large birds, and would rather die of starvation than attack small ones."

Cruelty

There once lived a strange creature called a basilisk, which was half bird and half serpent. It had a great crest on its head and along half of its back. It had a long tail, and wings like those of a bat.

All other animals, large and small, lived in fear of this creature with its venomous stare.

The basilisk only had to turn its gaze on any animal, a tiny bird or a huge elephant, to kill it.

No animal could escape that deathly gaze. The toll of victims increased by the day.

Then the animals decided to make their escape. Under cover of night they left their burrows and nests and went to a far-off wood.

At daybreak the basilisk set off as usual on its ruthless hunt. But it could not find a single living creature. In its rage, the basilisk turned its fatal gaze on the trees. And all the trees died. Then it stared at the grass. And the grass withered and died. And the beautiful forest became a desert.

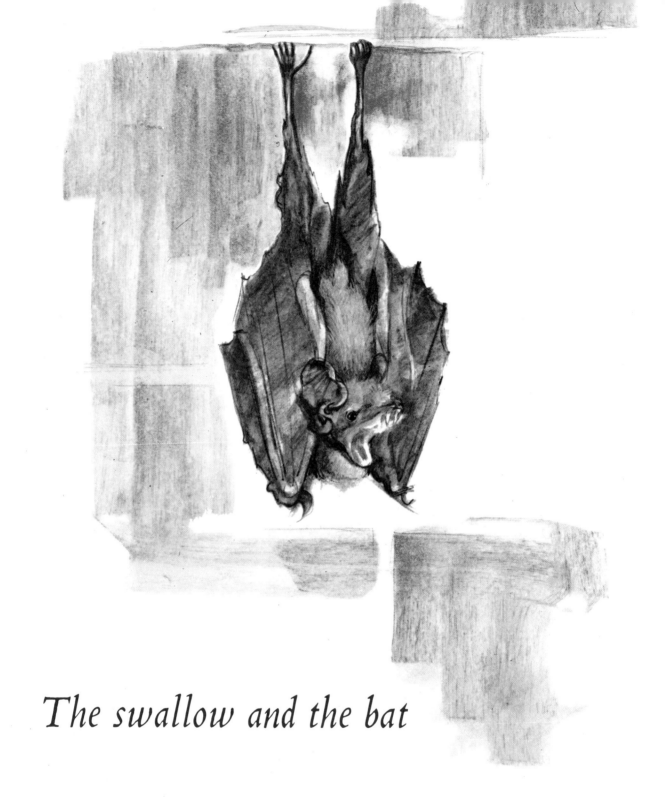

The swallow and the bat

The bat clung to the wall, just under the roof. He shielded his head with his wing from the powerful rays of the sun. He stayed like this all day until sunset.

When the sun went down, and the sky began to grow dark, the bat slowly lifted his head and looked around.

"At last," he exclaimed, "that hateful light has gone. Now I can open my eyes and fly."

A late swallow flew across his path as he left the wall.

"You know," she said to the bat, "you are like a vice which cannot stay where there is virtue. Virtue shines like the sun, and you hide from it for fear of becoming blind. The sun is like truth; if you look at it, it blinds you."

The lion
and the cockerel

With a thunderous roar, the king of beasts stretched his legs and set off at a run for the river, where many animals were to be found every day quenching their thirst.

Suddenly he heard a noise that frightened even him. It was an empty cart, pulled by a frisky horse, rattling over the stones.

Soon, when he had got over his fright, he set off again for the river. But this was a bad day for the lion. He had not gone much farther when he heard a cockerel crowing very close by.

He stopped again. The cockerel crowed again, more loudly. The lion
started to tremble. The cockerel, with its proud red comb, ran across his path
in the long grass. All the poor lion could see was the flame-red crest rushing
past crying, "Cock-a-doodle-doo".

Gripped by terror, he bounded back into the wood.

Macli

A very long time ago in Scandinavia, there lived a strange beast known as Macli.

It looked like a horse, but bigger. Its neck was not like the neck of a horse, nor were its enormously long ears like a horse's ears.

Macli fed on grass. It had to walk backwards when it grazed, because it had a very long upper lip, which would have covered the grass it was trying to eat if it had walked forwards.

None of its legs had joints, so it had to lean against a tree to sleep.

It could run with incredible speed, throwing its long straight legs forward.

No hunter could catch Macli. They had tried chasing it on horseback. They had even tried ambushing it in the places where it usually grazed—but all to no avail. This strange creature outwitted them all.

One moonlit night, some hunters came upon Macli sleeping. They were very surprised to see it sleeping upright against a tree, not knowing that its legs could not bend.

The hunters did not disturb the sleeping creature, and slipped away quietly.

The next morning, the hunters cut through the trunk of Macli's tree. In the evening they hid behind some bushes to see what happened.

After dark, Macli came to its usual tree and leaned against it to sleep. The trunk broke and the beast fell to the ground where the hunters seized it.

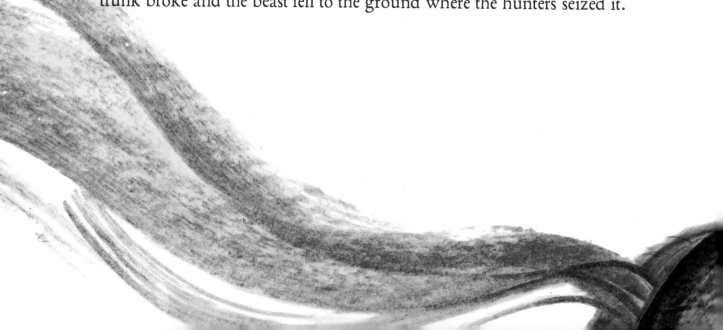

The kite

The kite was circling in the sky on outstretched wings, letting the wind carry him along high above the nest he had built at the top of a very tall beech tree.

When he returned to the nest, his hungry babies opened their mouths wide. But the kite gave each a sharp peck and looked at them angrily.

"I am giving you nothing to eat today," he said. "You are too fat. You must learn that the kite does not fly like other birds. He does not beat his wings furiously to stay aloft. Instead, he relies on the wind. If there is wind at a great height, the kite flies high. If the wind is blowing nearer the ground, the kite flies low. And when there is no wind, then the kite must use his wings. He must fly slowly upwards, using all his strength. If he is fat like you, he cannot do that. So that is why you will not eat today!"

The spider and the bee

One spring morning, a worker bee was flitting from flower to flower in search of pollen.

Suddenly he flew out of a flower straight into a spider's web. The spider had been hiding behind a leaf. Now he appeared, overjoyed at his catch.

"You are wicked!" cried the bee. "You spin your web to trap those who work."

The spider came nearer. The bee twisted himself round and tried to sting the spider.

The spider was too quick. He moved aside and escaped the sting, and he jumped on the bee.

"What right have you to judge me?" he asked the bee, gripping him tightly. "You call me wicked, but you are like deception itself; you have honey in your mouth, but poison in your tail."

Gratitude

One morning two hoopoos, a male and a female, did not feel like flying. They found they could not see very well. The sky was clear and bright, but the birds had a white mist over their eyes.

The fact is they were old and ill. The fine feathers on their wings and tails had begun to droop. They had started to look faded and dried up, like dead branches.

The hoopoos decided together that they would not even try to move, but would calmly wait for death, which surely would not be long in coming.

But instead their children arrived. One had happened to be passing and had seen that something was wrong. He fetched his brothers immediately.

When they were all there, one of them said, "We received the wonderful gift of life from our father and mother. They fed us and reared us and gave us all their love. Now they are ill, they cannot see and so cannot fly in search of food. We must take care of them until they are better."

When this bird had finished speaking, they all got to work. Some started to build a new nest. Some went in search of insects, some went to the wood to hunt.

Soon the new nest was ready, and the parent birds were helped to settle into it. To keep their parents warm, some of the young covered them with their own bodies, as a mother bird covers her eggs. And they cleaned and tidied their parents, pecking away the old dowdy feathers.

Finally the young birds who had been to the wood returned with herbs which bring back sight. These they gently rubbed over their parents' lifeless eyes. Soon the old birds opened their eyes and saw their children whose love and gratitude had cured them.

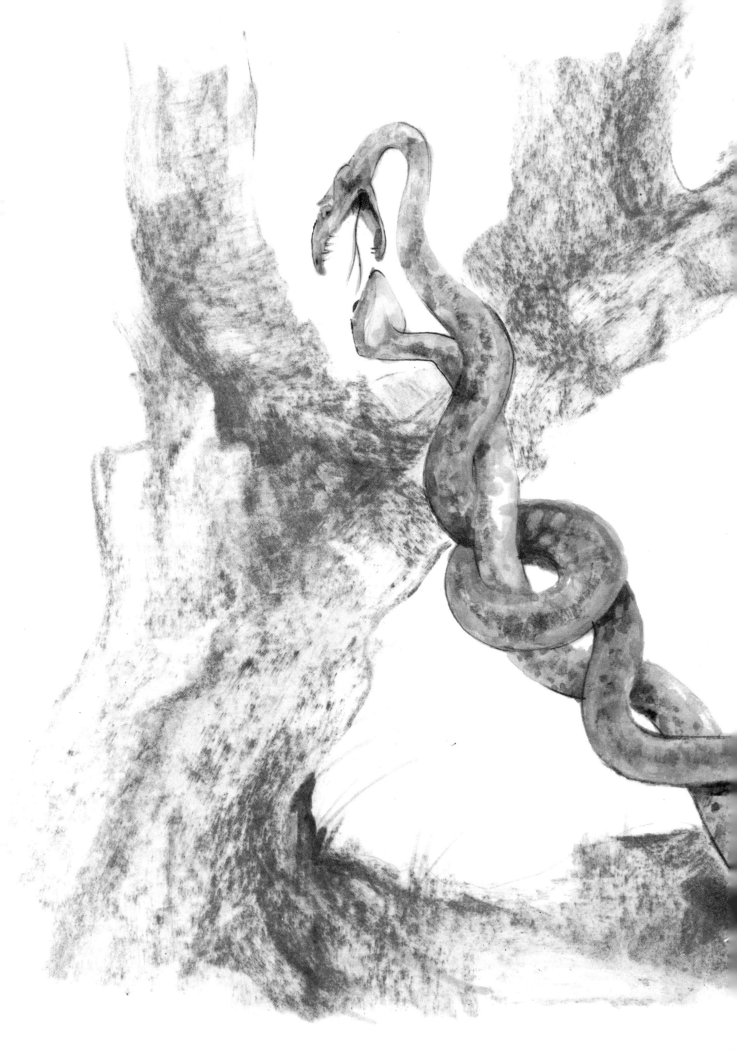

The viper

It was the season of love, and the female viper was waiting in the sun for the male viper.

She did not have to wait for long. The male approached the female with a slight rustle, and they coupled right away.

Then the female opened her mouth wide. When the male was about to move away, she seized his head in her mouth and killed him.

Soon it was time for the female to have her young. But the baby vipers were ready before she was, and they tore her open with their teeth. To be born more quickly the young had slain their mother.

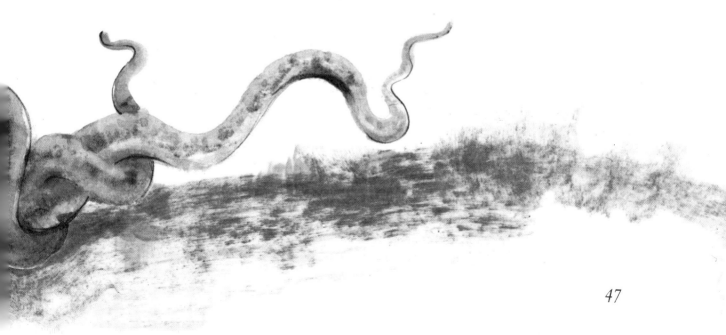

The falcon and the eagle

"The falcon," said the owl one evening, "is arrogant and proud. He wants to dominate and conquer all the other birds of prey. He is quite unsociable, preferring to be alone. On one occasion, a falcon flew so high to avoid others, that he met an eagle.

"You would expect him to have flown straight back down again. But no! Eagles allow no one to go near their nests; they are monarchs of the sky. But our falcon attacked the eagle."

"And who won?"

"No one knows. Next morning there was a large pile of feathers on the ground—some from the eagle and some from the falcon."

The lumerpa

In the lonely mountains of Asia there lives a fabulous bird. Its song is very sweet and its flight is majestic. Its body does not cast a shadow, because its feathers are so brilliant that they outshine the sun itself.

Even in death, this bird seems alive. Its body does not decay, and its feathers continue to shine as brightly as when it was alive.

But if anyone dares to pluck out a feather to make light for himself, the light is immediately extinguished.

This very rare bird is called the lumerpa. Like fame, the lumerpa continues to shine even after death.

The basilisk

In distant Cyrenaica, there is a dangerous creature called the basilisk. It is no more than twelve inches long, and has a white, crown-shaped mark on its head. With one hiss it puts all other creatures to flight, even other snakes like itself.

Instead of moving in a spiral like other serpents, the basilisk moves in a straight line with its head held high.

The basilisk is a terrifying animal. One day a horseman was returning home. Suddenly his horse shied to the side and neighed in terror. It had seen the basilisk. The horseman struck the serpent with his lance and killed it. But the reptile's powerful poison seeped up the shaft of the lance into the man's hand. Soon man and horse were dead too.

Then another basilisk came along. There was no one left for it to kill, so it breathed on the grass and the bushes. They shrivelled up and the stones were split apart.

The little birds and the cerastes

"Come and see!" shouted a little bird to his companion. "There are four worms on that leaf."

The worms were wriggling and writhing at the four corners of the leaf.

The second bird could not resist the temptation. He flew down towards the leaf to eat the worms.

The first bird watched his friend fly onto the leaf; then he heard him shout. At once he saw the ruffled feathers and the little wings beating in vain. Slowly the leaf wound itself round the helpless bird, and a terrifying cerastes was revealed hiding under the leaf.

The cerastes is a horned viper from north Africa. It has horns above each eye. When it wants to eat, it hides under a leaf so that only the horns show. It wriggles these about so that birds will mistake them for worms and be tempted near. When the birds swoop to seize the worms, the viper crushes them and eats them.

The amphisbaena

The mouse ran through the short tunnel and peeped out of a hole. The snake was still in front of the other hole where the mouse had slipped in. Every now and again it poked its head through the hole looking for the mouse.

The mouse waited for a suitable moment to escape. When he saw the snake exploring the hole in the sand again, he made his escape bid.

But what the mouse did not know was that this snake was the dreaded amphisbaena, which has two heads, one at each end. By the time the mouse realised, it was, of course, too late.

The worker bee and the drones

"Slackers!" shouted an old worker bee to the drones flying lazily round the hive. "You never do any work. Look at me working all the time. Look around. You will see that everyone is working. The ant, for example, thinks ahead to winter; she collects provisions throughout the long summer."

"That's a fine thing!" answered one of the drones who was growing tired of the worker's nagging. "The ant collects seeds to eat in the winter. So she stops crops growing by denying the soil the life that is in the seed."

The bite of the spider

The farmer was digging in his field. Suddenly a huge tarantula jumped out of a lump of earth.

"What a horrible spider!" exclaimed the farmer leaping back.

"If you touch me I will bite you," hissed the tarantula fiercely. "I warn you that my bite is poisonous. You will die in terrible pain."

The farmer looked at the spider. He knew that the spider must be lying because it was saying so much. He stepped forward and crushed the spider with his bare foot.

"Now let us see if you can make me die," he shouted.

The squashed spider did manage to bite the farmer's foot before it died. But the farmer had no reason to think he had been wrong about the spider's threat. In fact, the bite only smarted a little.

The bonaso

In Poland there lives an animal called the bonaso. It has a long mane on its neck, just like that of a horse. But the rest of the body is like a bull's. Its horns are not pointed like a lance, but curled back towards the head. Even if it butted anyone, the bonaso could not do any damage.

To defend itself, this wild harmless creature has to run away.

One day a group of hunters came upon a bonaso as it grazed peacefully in a meadow.

As soon as the animal saw the hunters, it shook its mane and fled. As it ran it left its droppings over a considerable distance.

The hunters soon gave up the chase and set off back along the way they had come. They were astonished to see that the bonaso's dung had scorched the grass where it had fallen. And one of the hunters said,

"Do you see that? In life every creature defends itself as best it can and in its own way."

The asp and the ichneumon

After being bitten by an asp, there is no remedy but to cut off the bitten part immediately. Nevertheless, this accursed animal has such a desire for company that it always goes about with one of its own kind, either male or female.

If, by any chance, one of the two happens to be killed, the other, with incredible speed, rushes after the killer. From that moment it has only one aim, to avenge its companion. And through its thirst for revenge it overcomes all adversity. If the killer is a soldier, the asp goes into the midst of the army without hurting anyone until it finds the one who is to blame. There is no obstacle that can stop the asp; it overcomes every difficulty, and only he who runs away very fast can escape from it, or he who throws himself over a stream of water.

The asp's eyes are sunk into its head. It has large ears, and it is its acute sense

of hearing, rather than its power of sight, that guides it as it moves along.

The asp's mortal enemy is a large rodent, called the ichneumon, which lives on the banks of the Nile.

When the ichneumon sees an asp near its nest, it rushes to the water's edge and plunges into the mud. Then it climbs out and lets the sun dry the mud clinging to it. It plunges into the mud once more, and again lets the mud dry in the sun. So it builds up layers of hard mud on its body, which acts like armour.

Then the ichneumon challenges the asp. It wards off the counter attacks, waiting for the right moment. When the asp opens its mouth wide to kill the ichneumon with its venomous teeth, the rodent, with one bound, leaps down its adversary's throat and suffocates it.

The siren

The wind had dropped, and the sails hung slack on the mast. The new moon barely penetrated the darkness as the ship rocked gently on the black mirror of water.

And the siren began to sing. The sailors heard a rustle like that of a gentle breeze. Then the music seemed to rise from the deep. The rustle became a voice sweeter than they had ever heard before. Soon the song had lulled them, one by one, into a sleep from which there is no waking.

In truth, when the sailors had fallen asleep on the still sea, the siren had climbed onto their ship, touched them one by one with her deadly hand, and they passed in their dreams from sleep to death.

The lion's revenge

The lion was asleep under a tree. He did not see
the hunters steal up and surround him.

A noise awoke him, but it was too late. There
was no escape.

One hunter grazed the lion's flesh. Another
inflicted a deep wound. Then, with a mighty
leap, the lion managed to climb into the tree. All
around men were everywhere, waiting for him
with pointed spears.

Then the lion raised his proud head, and gave
out a mighty roar. He leapt upon his first
attacker, determined to avenge the first blow,
even as he died.

The thirsty donkey

When the wild donkey went to the spring to drink, he found the water clouded by a crowd of ducks, who were chasing one another flapping their wings wildly.

The donkey was very thirsty. But he did not drink. Instead he stood aside patiently and waited.

At last the ducks went away. The donkey went back to the water. But it was still cloudy, and again he settled down to wait.

"Why doesn't he drink now?" a male frog asked a female frog. "That is twice he has come to the water and drawn back."

"Even if he is dying of thirst," replied the old female frog, "the donkey will not drink when the water is cloudy. He will wait forever for it to clear."

Liberality

The young eagle peered over the top of the nest and saw many birds flying about over the rocks below.

"Mother," he said, "who are those birds?"

"They are our friends," his mother answered. "The eagle lives alone, but he needs his court. Otherwise, over whom would he reign? These birds you see are our faithful courtiers."

The young eagle was satisfied, and he watched the other birds for a time. Then he exclaimed:

"Mother, those birds have stolen my food!"

"They have not stolen it," said his mother. "I gave it to them. Remember what I told you. The eagle is never so hungry that he cannot leave some food for his followers. Up here, they could not find any food for themselves. They would have to leave us to seek food farther down. He who maintains a court must be generous and tolerant. In exchange for their loyalty, he must satisfy his courtiers' hunger every day."

Justice

"There is no justice!" cried a mouse, narrowly escaping a weasel's claws.

"There is no justice!" shrieked the weasel, just escaping the claws of a cat.

"There is no justice!" mewed the cat, rushing up a tree to escape the barking dog below.

"You are right," said the owl. "But what is justice? Do you imagine it is a law?"

The mouse peeped out from his hiding place, the weasel poked his muzzle out of his burrow, the cat made himself comfortable between the branches, and the dog sat back.

"Justice," the owl went on, "is a virtue which may be compared to the queen bee. Have you ever looked at a beehive? The queen rules with reason, giving everyone his task to do. Some bees are sent off in search of flowers. Some have to work in the cells of the hive. Others fight off wasps or clean the hive. And some must look after the queen and be completely devoted to her. When the queen is old and cannot fly, the strongest carry her and the oldest care for her. If any bee fails to do his duty, he is punished with death."

The toad

The toad was fleeing from the glare of the sun. She hid among the stones, but became wedged and could not move. The sun's rays beat down on her. To protect her eyes she deflated herself and hid her head.

The enemy of virtue is like the toad. To win back virtue, he must be deflated and lose all arrogance.

The asp and the nightingale

The asp slithered towards the nightingale's nest. The parent birds were away, and the babies slept peacefully huddled close to each other.

From a nearby branch, the father bird saw the serpent, and flew to block its path.

"Stop," he begged. "Do not make a meal of my babies. If you spare them, I will give you the most beautiful song you ever heard." And with his sad mournful voice, he began to sing.

The asp was surprised by this interruption and stopped to listen. Then, so that it would not be bewitched by the beautiful music, which rendered even its venom powerless, it covered its ears with its tail and fled.

The spider and the swallow

Three times the spider had spun his silver web between two trees. And each time a mocking swallow skimmed past and broke it with her beak.

"Why can't you leave me in peace?" complained the spider. "Have I harmed you?"

"You are a wicked creature," replied the swallow. "That web you are spinning is a deadly trap."

"And what about you?" replied the spider. "Don't you always fly with your mouth open to catch insects? At least I work. I issue my silk and use my skill to spin a masterly web. My reward is the prey I catch in it."

The dragons and the ducks

The ducks soared up from the swamp. They had had warning of the dragons' attack.

From the air, they could see many serpents on the bank. They all had crests and large feet armed with claws.

The dragons decided to cross the swamp, to search for food on the other side. But they could not swim.

They wound themselves together, forming a shape like a large mat. They all held their heads above the water and floated across the swamp like a raft.

"Do you see that?" shouted the oldest duck. "Do you see what can be achieved if you are united?"

The panther

"Mother," shouted a young monkey, clambering up onto the branch where his mother was sitting, "I've just seen the most beautiful lioness!"

His mother peered down through the trees into the clearing.

"That is no lioness," she said. "Her legs are too long and her body too slender for a lioness. No, that is a panther. Look carefully at her coat with its black spots."

"She is *beautiful*," gasped the young monkey.

"Of course she is," replied his mother, "and she knows it as well as you do! All the animals run after her full of admiration. But they flee in terror when they catch sight of her face. It is a frightening sight!

"Take care, my son. The panther is crafty. When she sees she is being followed by admirers, she hides her face, so as not to frighten them away. Then, quick as lightning, she will turn and sink her teeth into the nearest victim and kill him."

The salamander

The farmer's hut was on fire, and all the animals fled from the yard.

Chickens, rabbits, turkeys, pigeons, turtle doves, the dog and the cat—they all watched with silent fear as the flames crackled and consumed the old dry wood.

Then a salamander appeared, crawling out from under a bush. She looked around quickly, then slipped into the flames.

"She does not feel the heat," said the rooster with feeling. "Her skin is insensitive to pain; she feeds on fire."

"But she will still burn," suggested a turtle dove, timidly.

"The salamander sheds her skin in the fire," stated the rooster. "She is the only creature who can.

"The salamander," he sighed, "is purified in the flames, and emerges rejuvenated and reborn. As for us, we would simply roast."

The fox and
the mysterious animal

There was a tree in the forest, just like any other tree, or so it seemed.

What no animal, even the wisest, realised was that an evil power dwelt in that tree.

To pass by that tree was to invite death. A brief hiss and the unfortunate creature was struck down. The animals did not understand it.

"An investigation is needed," they said. And they appointed the vixen to the task, as she was generally considered the cleverest and most artful.

The fox did not intend to take any risks. She turned for help to a bird whose life she had once spared. The bird immediately flew onto the tree in question.

A few days later, the fox was back to report her findings.

"On that tree," she said, "there is a strange animal, the strangest animal in the whole world. It is called the jaculo. When anyone approaches, it leaps from its branch like an arrow from a bow and passes straight through him. No one has ever seen its face or heard its voice. I propose that we move to another forest."

And off she went in search of another place to live, followed in silence by all the other animals.

The warmth of the heart

The two young ostriches were in despair. Every time they sat on their eggs, the weight of their bodies broke them.

One day they decided to ask for advice from their parents, who lived in another part of the desert.

They ran for many days and nights, and finally arrived at their old mother's nest.

"Mother," they said, "we have come to ask you how we should hatch our eggs. Every time we sit on them, they break."

Their mother listened to them, then she replied.

"You will have to use another kind of warmth."

"And what is that?" asked the young ostriches.

And their mother answered, "The warmth of the heart. You must watch over your eggs with love. Think about the tiny creature growing inside each one. Vigilance and patience will awaken them."

The young ostriches set off for home. When the female laid an egg, they watched over it with love and never relaxed their vigil. When they were both at the end of their strength, the egg began to creak and crack and break, and a little ostrich head peeped out of the shell.

The typeface used in this book is Monophoto Poliphilus.
It is a copy of a roman type cut by Francesco Griffo
for the Venetian printer, Aldus Manutius, in 1499.
It is an exact facsimile of Aldus's printed sheet.

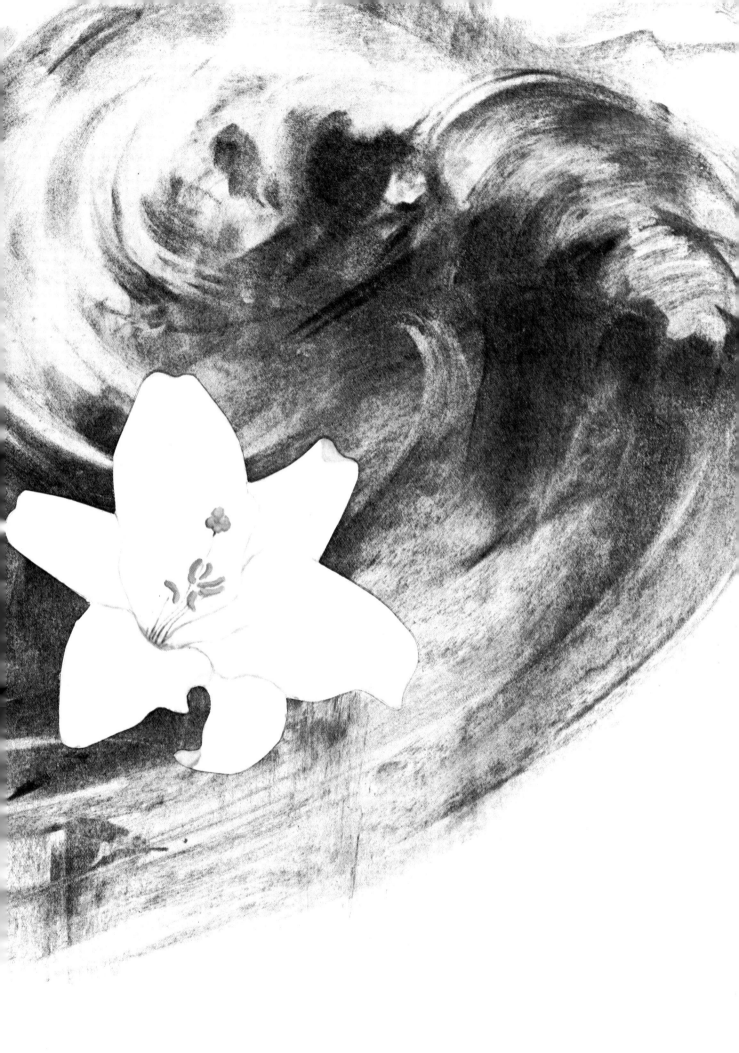